The Way It Really Was

THOMAS LOCKHART

PAGE PUBLISHING, INC.
Conneaut Lake, PA

First originally published by Page Publishing 2020

ISBN 978-1-64701-873-3 (pbk)
ISBN 978-1-64701-874-0 (digital)

Printed in the United States of America

Sylvester / Clementine Lockhart

Dedicated to mother and father, both being deceased. They were the best. They did all they could for all of our family. Mom and dad were both hard workers in their time, especially during plantation work. They were always busy planting, picking, and shopping cotton. They were easily the best gardeners you could find because they did it all. My parents worked hard; it was as if they knew I would be something in life. To mom and dad with love.

Sylvester Lockhart

Clementine Lockhart

Thomas Lockhart's Family.

The Bible says, "There is trouble on every side." It took a while for me to understand what the writer was saying. If you turn to the east, north, south. or west, there is trouble, and the only way you can beat it is to not get *involved*. People will tell you today, "I am staying out of the way." There are trials on every hand.

I say to young people today, the Kalamazoo Promise is available to you. Use it and get the best education you can. Don't let it pass you by. It could make the difference in your life. I know many of people who had the opportunity to use the Basic Education Opportunity Grant in the 1970s. They did not take advantage of, it and they put themselves in a position that did not help their life. It's the little things that causes us to miss out on the good things of life. I have procrastinated in my effort to finish this book. Should have finished it at least five years ago.

One of the judges at the court where I worked, after I had shared with her some things that happened in my life on the plantation where I lived, she said to me, "Tom, you're leaving your blessing in the streets." She said, "If you would put your story on paper, I will publish it for you for free."

This is the life story of Thomas Earl Lockhart, born and raised on a plantation in rural Isola, Mississippi, the son of Sylvester and Clementine Lockhart, the fifth child from the union of my parents. My mother and father married after my father had four children at that time. In all, the family consists of thirteen siblings all together. In those days, the government said every family farming or sharecropping would be issued forty acres of land and a mule. What we thought we had was not the case. We did have the forty acres and mule; however, it didn't turn out that way. This turned out to be what was known as sharecropping. My family would help plant the cotton, the soil beans, and all that went, along with planting and harvesting and picking the cotton by hand. We were trying to make enough money to support ourselves and to live a sustainable life. These were difficult times, having to work an entire crop season yet not enough money made to get out of debt or to support the family nor to be debt-free at the end of the season.

My father died at an early age of thirty-five years old. He was an independent man and taught his family to be the same way. He was beaten by eight white men while living on the plantation where we lived. He probably would have died an instant death if his four brothers hadn't gotten the message of what was happening at that time. When his brothers found out, they came running and did join in the fight. This was considered a race-related incident.

My father died five years after the fight; he was never the same again. When my father died, his older children left the plantation, along with my mother's four older children as well. This left my mother trying to fend for her five youngest. It was very difficult for her as she tried to maintain the land and care for the younger children. Things got worse instead of any better. It was noticeable that the owner of the land and the house we lived in would ride by almost every day, trying to buy something of value from my mother. She had to sell almost everything of value in order for us to survive from day to day. At that time, I was the oldest in the home while Mother worked in the field. In those days you grew up fast due to the circumstances around you.

One morning, while mother was working in the cotton field, I was charged with watching over the four younger siblings when we noticed people riding around our house on horsebacks and wearing white hoods on their heads. They were making the kind of noises that Indians made in the movies; they fired their guns through our windows. We crawled under the bed and stayed there until our mother came home. We were so afraid. I recall trying to keep the younger children from crying was a very difficult task. We were all in shock as these people posed as what was known as the KKK with masks on as they tortured us. We were so glad to see Mother when she arrived home. I tried to tell her the story and was told that I passed out while trying to do so. Mother knew this was the time for us to leave the plantation. She was afraid of what would happen next.

Mother acted with haste. She moved her family to a small town approximately eight miles from where we were. She met a man by the name of Mr. Pete Adams whom she later married. We called him Paw-Paw. He was six feet six inches tall; he was a man of business. He moved our family into a house immediately after meeting mother. The house was close to him, within walking distance, and like a dream come true. He taught me and the other siblings good work ethics and how to meet people of good character. He had somewhat of a dark side as well.

He was a moonshine runner. He was tied in with the sheriff of Sunflower County, Mississippi. We would be notified of when the revenue people would be present. He paid what we called shakedowns to the sheriff. He allowed me to deliver a white envelope to the sheriff every Monday after school. Paw-Paw ran the gambling house. He was the town's barber, and he owned a cafe on Front Street that my mother ran. She made the best sandwiches in town. My mother would buy thirty-five cases of rib to have a cookout in the park and sell every bone. She was a great cook and was given the reputation of being the best cook—one who could cook leather, and it would taste good.

Back then we considered it to be the good old days when people were allowed to carry what we called a tab at the restaurant. In other words, you could get what you wanted on credit and pay for it later. These were the good old days indeed because that does not exist any longer today in many places, or if at all. As I continue to tell my story, I want to encourage young men and women as they enter life to realize what their parents might have had to encounter to get to where they are today. As I continue to write, I also want to try to encourage young men and women to go after what they want in life. As I stated earlier, Paw-Paw taught me how to work at an early age. This was one

Siblings

Linda Lockhart

Dorothy Lockhart

Catherine Daniel
Ella Louise Lockhart
Hattie Mae Allen

Etha More Moffett

Darlene Lockhart

James Eddie Lockhart
John Edward Lockhart

Robert Lockhart

Michael Lockhart

After they moved to Chicago, IL, my brothers worked at Marshall Field and Company. Robert and John supported me greatly by sending clothes for me to wear while I was in college. All of my mother and father's children were all taught to love one another unconditionally. They also handed down other important life skills which made my sisters turn out to be good cooks. They learned from always being in the kitchen with our mother. My sister Hattie Lockhart Allen always made steak, mash potatoes and gravy for me when I came to visit. She worked for Jimmy Connor's mother for over 20 years. Talking about the famous Tennis player.

Zeus, the man of the house. Our family pet was a 128 pound Rottweiler and German Shepard mix. He was very protective of the house, my wife, and two kids. He didn't allow any trespassing.

of the best things that could have happened for me. He would have someone with a tractor break up land for gardening. My brother and I would row it up with shovels and hoes in order to get it ready for planting. People would ask Paw-Paw who plowed his garden, and we would just laugh, knowing that he was the plow. My first job was as a shoe-shine boy, earning thirty-five cents a pair of shoes. You had to split that with the owner of the building. We would say to our customers, "Go step in the mud and hurry back."

We always got a laugh out of that. From there, I worked at the cotton gin in Inverness, Mississippi, taking five to six hundred pounds of cotton from the gin's compress and rolling them to storage, getting them ready for shipment. The cotton gin was located in the heart of the city, close to where my family lived. It was considered a hazard to the health of individuals living in Inverness. It was located in a residential district instead of a commercial district. The NAACP was instrumental in trying to have the gin moved from within the city, but we found out that they, the leaders from within the NAACP, took a payoff.

Getting the gin removed from within the city was considered a bar chip for getting land for housing and for jobs so the younger population could have a place to stay and work and not be forced to relocate to other places. We marched on the city, with the march being led by the NAACP of Sunflower County, Mississippi. The first march was considered a success. However, they had taken the payoff and could not be trusted anymore. A friend and I went to speak with the attorney of the NAACP. He told us that we needed to get together on the matter. From there, I received a call from one of the leaders, stating that he didn't get much money but he would give me at least four thousand dollars. Now, for a young man with no job and no money and being twenty-six years old, I refused. My heart would not allow me to take the payoff. I felt this was dirty money and that I would be bowing down to man when I served a God who promised to supply all my needs. After that, I began to get threatening letters from someone who worked for a specific company that many of the individuals worked for. They were trying to frighten me to make me move out of town. When I told my mother of the threats, she made a way for me to leave Inverness, Mississippi, in 1983.

At that time my mother was sickly, and I would hate to leave her, being the oldest at home. I left her my car, a 1976 Pontiac Brougham. I knew that I would make it in life. My intuition from God allowed me to see that there were things awaiting me in life. I wanted my mother to be able to get to the doctor and to have transportation for the rest of the family. However, my sister Darlene totaled the car two weeks after I had left home. I came to Kalamazoo Michigan, wanting to prove myself right away. I didn't know anyone there. I recall applying for a job at Kmart store. I got a call on Tuesday afternoon. The caller asked if I was Tom.

I replied, "No, this is Thomas."

I was not used to being called Tom. Whoever called hung up on me. The spirit of God spoke and said it was someone calling me for a job. I got down on my knees and began to pray to God that if that was someone calling me for a job, please let them call again. About twenty minutes later the telephone rang again, and the same person was calling back. She asked me what I liked to be called, and I told her Thomas, and she stated that she was having a bad day, and if I wanted the job, it was mine. She told me to be at the job the following day and start working.

I asked the Lord to allow me to get home with 150 dollars a week, and he did. Then I asked to get home with three hundred a week, and he did. I did not come short of my blessings; I just wanted to have something of my own. I have trusted in God's word for as long as I could remember who he was. I didn't even have a winter coat when I came to Michigan. If anyone knows anything about the state of Michigan, you know it gets really cold. My paycheck continued to progress; my check increased to three hundred dollars a week while working at Kmart. I did not come short of God's blessings because I trusted God's word.

I really didn't have much when I came to Kalamazoo, Michigan; however, I knew God and trusted in him. I didn't even have a winter coat. I had to learn the hard way that winter in Michigan was very different from winter in Mississippi where I came from. I didn't have any transportation either, did not know how to ride city transportation. It was here at Kmart on Gull Road, I saw a Blue Light Special going on, and there was a beautiful young lady in charge of the Blue Light Special. She caught my eye right away. Her name was Zilda Moore. After I met her, she gave me rides home after work. We fell in love and got married in 1991. She was instrumental in helping me to understand the Michigan way of life. We are still happily married after twenty-six years.

Before my father died, we had a great life. We grew most everything we ate from the table. We had our own livestock, had hogs, chickens; also my father and brothers were hunters. They fished in order to provide a good life for the family.

We would store things for the off seasons. For instant potatoes, sweet potatoes white potatoes were stored with cornstalks and hay to keep them for the winter months. Meat was stored very differently from how it is done today. Meat from a hog would be laid out on the smokehouse floor. Salt would be poured on it for curing purposes, and when cured enough, it would be hung from the ceiling and brushed with liquid smoke. From that we carried what we called salt-pork sandwiches to school for lunch. You had to carry a greasy bag up until your lunch. This was truly a way of life back then. We had chicken on the yard in those days. They were ordered by what we called a crate. We also called the chickens biddies because they were so small when they first arrived.

We had more than enough until things changed after Father died. Very little education had taken place in my family at that time. None of the older siblings had successfully attended school. No one had graduated from high school at that time. This really concerned me, and I thought this would be a good time for a change within the family. I then finished high school, went to college at Mississippi Valley State University, and received a bachelor of science degree in teaching. I tried to encourage the ones that followed after me. However, they did try. All of them enrolled in college but did not graduate. I knew this would make life easier for them to get a better job.

I played baseball in high school at Gentry High School. From there I was recruited by Mississippi Valley State University. I injured my rotator cuff my sophomore year. I became so confused and did not return to school the following year. The coach was fired that year for telling the players to take their uniforms to the president's office and lay them on his desk. He wanted to play more games and thought this would change things. It got him fired.

I began to play baseball when I moved to Kalamazoo in 1982 on a city league with Coach Steve Powers. Steve was impressed with my play. He had a professional scout to come out to our practice one day. The scout was impressed also. He asked me how old I was.

I told him, "I'm twenty-eight."

He said, "You are more than capable, but the organization won't allow me to sign you."

This was the end of my baseball career. I want to say this primarily to the younger people out there. If there is ever a time in your life when you feel alone, remember there is always help around you. My faith taught me that there is a God, a supreme being who says in the Holy Bible, in the book of Philippians, the writer Paul says, "But my God shall supply all my needs according to his riches in glory."

I have come to know that God owns it all. However, there must be that trust and faith that you must have in him to know that he will do what he says. There were times in my life that I wanted things that my mother could not afford. I stood on the side of our house and cried because she didn't have it to give to me. A voice entered my head. It said, "If your father was alive, you could have what you want." Then I felt what I called an angelic voice that said, "You have to be Daddy now." I said that to say to anyone out there, who may be struggling the way that I was, that you can make it if you put your mind to it and get going with it. Don't give up when things get tough. If you can learn to put your trust in God, he will guide you through it. In other words, if God brings you to it, he will bring you through it.

I would suggest to anyone who reads this book to read these scriptures from the Holy Bible: the book of Proverbs chapter 3, especially verses 5–6. Verse 5 says, "Trust in the Lord with all thine heart;

lean not unto thine own understanding." Verse 6, "in all thy ways acknowledge him, and he shall direct thy path." I am speaking from experience that I have lived in my own life. Believe me, I could not have made it to where I am without the Lord on my side. I can even say, where would I be without God's blessings? I would simply be lost. I became the father of my life at a very early age when I really needed someone to be there for me. I simply had to recognize that I was in between a rock and a hard spot because I wanted to be independent and found ways to make things happen that needed to happen in my life.

The wisdom and knowledge I gained by trusting and having faith in God pulled me through. God didn't promise to make me rich, but he did say that he would supply all my needs. He showed me that I must take action in order to progress in life. It helped me to become a harder worker than ever before. It paid off to the point that I was able to work a job that gave me pension and saved enough to take care of my family. I am not saying that God will set things at your disposal, but instead, you must take the necessary action in order to attain what you need. We would still be sitting at the back of the bus if Rosa Parks hadn't refused to give up her seat to a white person back then or if Dr. Martin Luther King didn't lead the marches in the many cities he led.

My Bible teaches me that God gives us the strength to get the things we need. Philippians 4:13 says, "I can do all things through Christ who gives me the strength." We must believe this and treat it this way. Life is not a flower bed of ease. You are going to go through some trials in life. I have had many kinds of jobs but was determined to make it in life. I had to learn to work really hard. I started to work at the Youth Center School after leaving Kmart in Kalamazoo, Michigan. I continued to ask God for more and more for my needs or one who might say to supply my needs in life.

From there, I started working at the juvenile home where I absolutely loved working with the young people and with people in general. I saw and felt the need to help wherever I could. The super-intendent allowed me to take children to other juvenile facilities to play ball and to enhance their social growth. This was an exciting time in my life and in the life of the children. The one thing that amazed me the most about working with the children was the respect they gave to me when they knew that they were being loved. I never lost a child when we went other places.

One thing I always observed was, these children knew when they were being loved, and they always gave it back. A recording artist wrote a song in the seventies that said, "It's good loving somebody when somebody loves you back." Most of these young people had been deprived of love. They loved me so much they would let me know if anything was going on in the building that I needed to know. They would ask me if I would be at work on any given day because they were planning on jumping staff or causing problems for staff but would only do this if I wasn't there. I didn't think about the question until they had acted.

As a worker, I treated all the children the same. I didn't care what the charges were; my job was to work with them to assist them in their daily routine. I treated them according to the policies of the institution. I feel to this day that I can get children to work within their means or up to their capacity despite of their disposition. Everyone can feel the love that's on the inside of them.

Working for the Kalamazoo County Juvenile Court, I made recommendations and wrote reports for judges and referees. That included institutional, foster care, family placement, and more. We called these placements "loveless placements" because what the children needed was right at home. The court built a state-of-the-art juvenile home, with treatment facility as an alternative placement. Many of the young people who were being sent away to placements can now remain in the home and work on the issues with their families. This was one of the best things that could have happened.

If you happen to read my story and are in a situation as such, please by all means take advantage of anything that can assist you in making any changes you need to make in your life. No one can change you; you have to do that yourself. Take advantage of what's put before you that will help you to make the changes you need to turn things around in your life. One of the most important things I learned in life was respect for myself and then others in and around me. I not only learned from family but from others within the small community which I lived.

My mother, being a single parent at the time, was a strong woman who was respected by her own and by the community as well. I worked long hours to assist in supporting our family. I had to grow up faster than I wanted to. I mentioned earlier in my writing about my gambling habits. I learned to gamble from the older men in town. We could walk into the cafe and do what the older did if you had the money.

The town where I lived was a very small place of less than five thousand people. This was in the mid nineteen seventies when I attended college at Mississippi Valley State University in Itta Bena, Mississippi. I would come on the weekend to gamble, waiting for those who worked all week in the cotton fields—whether planting, picking, or ginning the cotton, getting the cotton ready for ship-ping to the compress for the market. They wanted to see me because they wanted to beat the college boy. They called me the smart boy; they were proud of me. Not many of us attended college in this little rural town. We played pool, shot dice, and played cards.

There was not very much more for the young people to do there. We played lots of sports. I believe I mentioned earlier in my writing that my stepfather was what we called a bootlegger in the town. Meaning he bought and sold moonshine, or people called it "coin whiskey." This took place at our home and at the cafe. There were people knocking on our door at every time of the night. This was cheap whiskey illegally brewed by many who found the time to utilize the trade to make money. When I say cheap, you could buy from a quarter shot up to a pint of whiskey. You could sell the gallon for fifteen to seventeen dollars. I was trained to transact all these methods and more. What I mean by more is that when I started col-lege, I met others who smoked and sold marijuana.

My first investment in marijuana was 150 dollars in what was called a brick of marijuana. You could make 3,000 dollars profit from 150 dollars selling what we called nickel-and-dime bags. This was a five and ten-dollar bag. This started in my hometown and followed me to the university where I lived.

In order to make money, you had to lose lots of sleep when participating in this activity. Since many people came in and out of our home; no one really paid attention to what I was doing… There was always traffic at the house. I was mainly a street person. I woke up in the morning headed for the streets because there was money to be made out there. I sold marijuana for over five years. People would come from all the surrounding small towns to buy from me—whether on the streets or on the school playground.

With all the activity I was involved in, I gained the name *Tom Slick*. When I was in the street, this name seemed to have been all right, but I began to realize that others saw me as someone that I was not. I can't forget that after one Friday night, I came home to play pool and to gamble in dice and cards. I had won some money and was on my way back to school the next day to a football game. As I traveled up highway number three, I observed the police flashing his light and waving for me to pull over. I had a brick of marijuana under the seat. As the policeman came to the driver's side of the car, he asked my name and said I was driving over the line and asked if there was a reason for that. I told him I was drinking some orange juice, which I loved to drink by the quart. He asked where I was going, and I told him back to school to a football game; and the reason I was over the line, I was trying to open the orange juice. He asked if I smoked or had any marijuana on me, and I said no. Only if he had searched my car, I would have been in big trouble.

This was a time in my life that things began to spiral out of control. I had torn my rotator cuff while practicing baseball, and my scholarship was in question. I had to figure out how to get through school on my own or without going into debt. I was able to figure out how to beat the system by living on campus without having to pay for room and board.

Life on campus became miserable for me. Many times, a friend would give me his meal ticket to eat at the cafeteria. His name was Alvin Butler from Indianola, Mississippi, where we both attended high school together. Many of these days I had no food to eat; I only drank water. However, it didn't have to be that way, but I was determined to be independent and didn't want to tell my mother or stepfather, knowing they would have made a way. There were times when me and my friends would go to the store, take steaks and any other meats we could to keep from being hungry. If we had gotten caught, it would have made things worse for us. These were some of the most difficult times, but I made it and many times at the expense of others.

My older brothers, Robert and John, who lived in Chicago, Illinois, provided clothes for me while I attended high school and college. This was a true blessing for them to think of me the way they did. They were pleased that I had stayed in school and got to the point of graduation, being the first of thirteen to finish high school and then finish college.

After I finished college, I could not get a job in the school system where I lived because you had to pass what the state of Mississippi called the National Teachers Examination. After taking the test twice and failing, I became frustrated and would not take it again. I moved to Kalamazoo, Michigan, with the mother of my first child, and from there I began to work at the retail store Kmart as a stock person. This was my first job in Kalamazoo. I was able to pay the bills, then things began to get better.

With a bachelor's degree, I got a job as a teacher at the Juvenile Home school through the Kalamazoo Valley School District. This was an opportunity to meet others of whom I felt comfortable to be around. Finally, I applied at the juvenile court and did get the job after the ninth or tenth time I applied. I was very frustrated after applying for the job so many times and not getting it. I am now on the professional path that I wanted. I worked so hard to prove myself; it was not easy, but I refused to fail. I wanted my critics to know that I could do the job. I said that to say this, whenever you put your mind and spirit into whatever you're doing, it will work out. The route that I followed was a spiritual route involving the job.

Young people, please hear this, I quote from the King James Bible here. The Bible teaches that "if a man works, he eats." It makes good sense to me. My father was a hardworking man; Mother was a hard-worker. This was passed on to the children. This is the idea that we train up a child in the way they should go. They might shun away from it, but they will return. It's called "planting the seed." The Bible also teaches, "Little children, obey your parents that your days may live long on this earth." "All things are possible if we believe."

You know, sometimes the things we need don't always start at home. The best part about life is that what you need to make it in life is on the inside of you, your conscience. God has equipped each of his children with a conscience that lets us know when things are good or not good for us. There will always be a spirit of good and evil in our lives. If we want to be successful, we must choose to do good and not evil. The Apostle Paul wrote in the Holy Bible, "When I try to do good, evil is always present." The good thing is that we have a choice. We can always choose which way we want to go.

While working at the juvenile court, many of the young people I worked with would say to me, "Mr. Lockhart, I make more money than you, and you work five days a week."

I would say to them, "You may but I don't have to be watching or looking over my shoulders all the time, running from police." I would tell them that it's hard to win. You can't beat the police. They have what we call people who inform them on what's going on out in the streets. One good informant is better than a hundred police. They could be your best customer. Somewhere along the way, you will hear a still small voice telling you the right way to go. That thing called a conscience, which I talked about earlier in my writings. For the Bible says "Greater is he that is in me than he that is in the world." It is simply referring to the things that will make life better for you if you follow his way rather than the way of the world. Drinking, smoking, doing all kinds of drugs will destroy your life, land you in jail or prison, separate you from your family. It will cause your heart to bleed. These things will cause you to go down the path of wrongness and may or may not recover.

The good part is that you can recover, but that means you have to change the way you think and the way you do the things that you do. When I made the changes in my life that really mattered, I had to get away from my so-called friends. There were some places I used to go that I couldn't go anymore. The things I used to do, I had to stop doing.

The Bible says, "If any man be in Christ Jesus, he's a new crea-ture. Old things are passed away; behold, all things are become new." I simply decided to change the way I lived. I believe the way of life can help to turn a man/woman's life around, if you want to change. You don't have to be super smart to make it in life. However, you simply need to be willing. You don't have to make a huge paycheck from month to month.

The Apostle David says, "But my God shall supply all your need according to his riches in glory by Christ Jesus." I want you to know he owns it all. He will show you the way to help yourself, if you really want to change. I used to hear the elders say, "If you make one step, God will make two. Despite what happened to Mom and Dad in life, you can still be successful, if you want to." Things didn't get much easier when I put time in on the job. The closer I got to retire-ment, things seemed to get more difficult. Trials start showing up.

At that time, I got sick on the job and could not work up to the capacity of the past This resulted in my retirement. I retired at the age of fifty-five years old. This was a time to think about what I wanted to do after my retirement.

To this day I still love children and families. This, I can say, is *embedded* in my heart. I have always wanted to be my own person and not to follow after any and every thing. I first learned to do what is best for myself and those around. I believe that life will always return to you what you put into it.

Another blessing I said I would never do or would be was to be a pastor in God's church. I was wrong. I pastored for a total of twelve years and really came to love it.

Throughout my life I learned that love is the most important part of my life. I learned to love after what happened to my family on that plantation. I carried bitterness and hatred around with me for many years. I found out that I could not shake it. It took God to remove it from me.

For any young and older person who may have the opportunity to read this book and may be going through the trials of life, there are times when the best thing you can do is let go of anything that may be holding you back, or anything that may cause you not to be all that you can in this life. Life can be so beautiful, if we allow it. You may feel that your father was not there for you; alcohol or drugs might have entered into the family. Don't let any failures of life hinder you.

Hold your head up high so that you can see where you want to go and give it all you got, and things will work out in your life. You can be whatever you want in your life. Don't let anyone or anything deny you of being what you want to be or doing what you want to do. You can say the sky is the limit. All you have to do is get started and set your mind to whatever you want to do.

My story is that, I can do all things that God has willed in my life. Don't be a statistic in the wrong way. Too many people get caught up in the way of the world.

I can tell you that it could have been me. I see people standing by the way side, not knowing which way to turn. It could have been me. By the grace of God. I was fortunate enough to see my way out. I believed in the word of God, in which my parents gave to me as a child, and that's what sustained me.

Just a little food for thought: I never dreamed of being where I am in life today. I was told by certain teachers in school that I wouldn't make it, but they were not in charge of my life. The ones they suggested would make it became alcoholics or drug addicts.

I can say that no one has control of mine or your life. I used to hear my mother say, "Your life is what you make it." I miss Mother so much. She would never say what her children would do but was always there to support if trials came. I loved to hear her say many of the sayings we shared in order to reference life. She would say to me, "Son, a quarter of yours is better than a dollar of someone else's." If I asked her to borrow money, she would say, "Borrowing make enemies. Let's me and you stay friends." Another one was she would tell people when they were trying to get over on her. She would tell them, "I am not the little girl that brought the pumpkin to town. I'm the one who sold it."

She simply made people laugh. Mother was not an educated lady but full of motherly wit. She would say, "Boy, I've been around the ham bone and tasted all the meat." She could not even read at the age of forty-five. My sister, Dorothy, taught mother to read. My family is getting smaller as the days go by. Three of the step-children are no longer with us, and four of the nine of my mother and father's union has passed away as well.

I've always considered myself to be a late bloomer. Seeing that maturity came late in life for me, I was blessed with many talents, like singing. I was always told that I have a beautiful voice. I was a talented baseball player, a good football player, and good in basketball. Many times, I felt that I didn't have anyone around me to push me or to help me achieve my goals. I spoke of my elder brothers who moved away from home when I was ten years old. However, my high school coach, Jack Thompson, helped me along as best as he could. He would bring me home after baseball practice. He wanted me to make it in professional baseball. He drove me and a friend, Lloyd Galloway, to Mississippi Valley State University to sign our letter of intent. He was like a father figure to me. I have the utmost respect for him to this day and love him as a father. I continue to have con-tact with him to this day. He was an English teacher at Gentry High School where I attended.

As my thoughts are coming to a close, I can't help but think about how young men are so enticed with having children these days. The average one, of whom I had the pleasure of working with over the thirty years in the court system, has about five children. I want to sug-gest something to you. Put your thoughts toward an education. You want to be able to care for any children you bring into this world. Set some goals for yourself and work toward reaching those goals. You can do it if you try. You, like anyone else, can do good in life if you focus. We live in a society where we have lost respect for women. It does not have to be that way. My parents taught me to be very careful when it comes to hurting others' feelings. Sometimes we can lead or mislead others into situations that cause them to fail in life. My mother would say, "It's just nice to be nice. If you can't say something nice about someone, don't say anything."

Many of our young people are having children at a record high, and the fathers are nowhere to be found, causing the young children to have very little structure in their lives or any at all. Any man can be a daddy, but it takes a real man to be a father. I want young men and women to count up the cost of what you're doing in life. Think about others around you and how you affect other people. If you make the mistake of having a child out of wedlock, please think about what you have and try to do what's good for everyone involved. Back in the days when I was growing up, if you got a girl pregnant, your parents saw to it that you married that person. You took care of that child and that mother. You didn't run away.

We are running away from our responsibilities today. Young girls get pregnant today. They want to move out of their parents' home, get one child, then another in order to get whatever assistance they can, and the beat goes on.

Today there are too many baby mommas. I have to see young men that I work with in the juvenile system. They see me out and about and say hello to me or give me a hug. Somewhere in the conversation, we talk about family. I always ask the question of how many children you have, and every one that I've ask has said five. I want to encourage our young people to think about your situation and always remember that you can overcome many of the situations you are in or that you put yourself in. We all make mistakes in life, but they can be overcome.

Here in Kalamazoo, Michigan, where we live, many of the well-to-do businessmen and women got together and came up with what we, or they, call the Promise. It allows students who live in the city of Kalamazoo, Michigan, to attend college for free, but you must live in Kalamazoo. I do know that this has been a blessing for my family, to both of my children being birthed here in Kalamazoo. We are saving in many ways because of the Promise.

Sometimes children don't want to attend college right out of high school. My son was one of those. He said to me that "I have twelve years to use the Promise." He wanted to pursue a rapper's contract but with no road map of how he's going to get there. It took much counseling to get him to see that a bird in the hand is better than one in the bush. He has come to his senses and is attending college and doing great. Many people have moved to Kalamazoo because of the Kalamazoo Promise. The city has grown because of this special gift to its people. President Obama came to speak at Kalamazoo Central High School in 2012.

The student wrote an essay that involved other high school students, with Kalamazoo Central being the winner that allowed President Obama to come. What an exciting time for our city. Had to mention that the president was in town.

Now to get back to my writing. I always try to encourage young men to stay in school, learn to work, and to become family-oriented. There are many times you see too many young men on the streets shooting dice, gambling, or you may say breaking the law, and not setting a good example for the younger ones to follow. I had to learn to carry myself in a way that would be pleasing to other in the community where I lived. I realized that I was on my way to becoming a statistic, referring to doing something to get into trouble, go to prison or jail, realizing that things were different for a black man than for a white man in our society when it comes to the law or crimes being committed.

All I'm trying to say is that one must know what he or she is confronted with as we travel along this pilgrimage journey. Some of the words that I heard around my house was that trouble is so easy to get into but hard to get out of. I find that to be so true. I was not one who stayed in trouble, but I was a lookout one Sunday night when three friends and I broke into a cafe. We used what we call a crowbar to break into the business. I was really the lookout person.

We took seven hundred dollars from the music box and pool table. Somehow our names were with the sheriff of the town. He questioned all of us involved and let us go. My stepfather asked me if I knew anything about what happened. I told him no. The sheriff told my stepfather that I was the black child he had seen, that I looked him in his eyes and convinced him that I had nothing to do with the B and E (breaking and entering). I had just turned eighteen years of age and would have been considered an adult, was in my senior year of high school. This could have been a deadly blow. My future plans, college, baseball, my reputation could have all been put in jeopardy. My mother was the kind of person who would stand with her child, no matter what the charge. She said to me, "Son, we'll get through this."

The fact that I was a decent child, student, etc., my school coun-selor came to court with me with my pastor and said good things about me that helped get me out of trouble. My stepfather said, "Son, if you had told me when I asked you, it wouldn't have gone this far." I felt so ashamed of myself after getting through all of what happened. We buried the $700.00—plus dollars on the railroad track. One of the young men involved, his mother made him go and dig it up once the police was told we did it. After this incident in my life, I was able to get on the right track and stayed on the good side of life. Though there were times when things got tough for me. I felt as though I was out on an island alone, especially my last two years of college. I was a five-year college student to receive a four-year bachelor's degree. It took me extra time because my focus was not on education alone. I wanted to have a good time while attending school.

Certainly, college can be the best life one can live. Think about it. Meals are paid for. All one had to do was bag up your laundry and drop it off to be washed and return to pick it up. It was not that good at home for me. I had chores at home. Sometimes it's easy to get caught up in things not healthy for us. Nobody said the road would be easy. I always believed if God brought me to it, he would bring me through it.

When things get tough in life, there is an old saying that says, "the tough get going." I submit to you today, there will be times when it seems like nothing is going your way. Your faith and your trust will bring you through. By the way, my faith is in God. I can tell you as I write to you in my story that I know that he is real because of the many ways he has shown himself to me. I want you to think about this: your daily life consists of a test of your faith and your trust in God. He showed me that only I could determine whether I pass the test or not. What I am trying to say is, don't let anyone deter-mine how your day will go. There is so much trouble, or shall I say temptation, in our surroundings it can be difficult sometimes. Don't let those times distract your attention. The Bible teaches us, there is trouble on every side.

Being a teenager can be the most difficult time of your life if you are not focused. Mother would say, "You've got the world in your hands," to her children. She would say, "Trouble is easy to get into but hard to get out of." I never thought of life that way until trouble came. However, that was certainly the truth. It is so easy to take something from someone else, but having to pay the consequences for it can be very difficult.

My life has been a most interesting one. Many things have transpired in the sixty-three years I've been in this world. One of the biggest things I am battling at the age of sixty-three is within the church. I thought that the older that people became, they would be trying to get closer to God. This does not seem to be true for most of us who say that we have been saved, baptized, and received salvation through confessing in the belief in Christianity or whatever you believe. It does not seem to be headed in that direction. We are struggling whether to follow God or man. Man seems to be doing his best to assist people in following the creature rather than following God, the creator. We must understand that man will deceive you; he will mislead you in order to show himself. I have seen in my lifetime when man takes to that approach. God will uncover him to say that God will show you to other people, show your behavior to other people.

As a Christian, a believer in God the Father, God the Son, and the Holy Ghost, to explain that this is the nature of God, they work three in one and one in three. They are equal in power and authority. Christianity is what has worked for me and my family. My faith and my trust in God are what have kept me on the right path. I can sing the old hymn, "We came long ways, Lord, a mighty long ways. I've had hard trials, been in the valley, had to pray night and day, and that's what brought me through." If there is anything that families need to do in this day and time, it is to pray.

The Bible teaches that we should always pray and not give in to the enemy. Prayer will bring about a change in our lives. If a family is to be strong and tightly knitted, there must be such as love, peace, happiness from within the family. As a man/ woman, we should do the best we can to show love within our home, which will be passed on to our children so that they pass it on to their children in building up the family for future generations to come. Sometimes it can be so hard for families to beat generations of abuse, suffering, and discomfort within the family because the ones before them did not pay much attention to the family function before them. I love to refer to the Bible when it comes to my life.

In Acts 16:16–31 Paul and Silas were in prison. An earthquake came and reduced the jail to rubble. The jailers came looking for them and screamed out, "Is everyone all right?" They said, "We are here." The jailers were so amazed that they were alive and the fact that they were saved from the storm. They said to Paul and Silas, "What must we do to be saved?" Paul and Silas said for them to call on the name of the Lord, and they shall be saved. They said not only shall you be saved but your household shall be saved.

Young men and women, as head of your household, you should be able to pass on something good to those who come after you. We should live our lives in a manner that will be beneficial to those who follow you. If the family puts forth the effort to carry on in a loving, caring, affectionate way, the family will change. If you don't put anything in to the family or anything else, you won't get anything out. In most cases, you simply have to put something in, in order to get something out.

You can't get money out of the bank if you don't put some in. You can't go to the grocery store and get groceries if you can't pay for it. It's hard to get an education if you do go to school. Reminds me of a jailhouse lawyer. You learn a little something in jail, but it won't allow you to get paid. A self-taught teacher can't get a job in the community. So many of our young people today are going on the internet, getting degrees but cannot get a job because many of them are not accredited, which means no one will hire you without an accredited degree.

The internet may seem to be the easiest way to get a degree, but somehow it holds you to the fact that the easiest way is not always the best way. It's like taking your car to what we call a "shade tree mechanic." You pay less money for the job, but you will have to take the car to someone else to have it repaired. I said that to say this: you might as well put in the time and effort in school to get what you need rather than take the shortcut. The shortcut will always do just what is called, allow you to come up short. There is no need for any of us to come up short. I have been thinking about writing this book for ten years, been procrastinating, but have finally decided to finish it up.

The Lord blessed me with many talents. I have a beautiful tenor voice. Many call it an angelic voice, as I sing in church and have been told by many that they wish they could sing like me. I am very athletic and should have played professional baseball, as mentioned earlier in my writing. I was recruited by Cincinnati Reds in high school.

Went to college at Mississippi Valley State University in Itta Bena, Mississippi, in what is still considered the SWAC (Southwestern Athletic Conference). I tore my rotator cuff in the tenth grade. There were many trials and tribulations that came upon me, but even from there, I made it.

I was down to my last dime many days, but I made it. My so-called friends turned their backs on me, but I made it. I didn't know what the next day would bring, but I hung in there. I heard mother say, "If you do good, good will follow you, the same with the bad." When I say "I made it," it was by the grace of God that he kept me; by the grace of God, he never left me. I endured my afflictions because God never left me. I can say today, through it all, I've learned to trust in Jesus. I've learned to trust in God.

Young people, your life should depend on at least these two things every day, and that is a test of your faith and a test of your trust. Is my faith strong enough to carry me through the day? The Bible says it's impossible to please God without faith. Do I trust in him, in his word? And if I have my faith in order, my trust in order, I will make it. God said he will supply my needs according to his riches and glory. He owns everything. He's not going to send you a car down here, but he has made away for you to earn it. He said, "If a man works, then he can eat." He's the reason why we have what we have. We don't own anything down here. If you don't believe me, try taking something with you when you leave. We came into this world with nothing, and we will leave with nothing.

If there is anything that I want to happen for me before I leave the world, I would like to pastor again in the sense that I would have only the amount of leadership to grow the church, the winning of souls for God/Christ, and not treating people as if though they are slaves, not wanting to have people to worship me instead of God. For I know that if I put myself in such a position, God will move me out of the way so that his people can see him. People are using God's church to dictate to God's people. Many people don't realize that God had made us free, moral beings. And if we believe in him, he will supply our needs.

I have been blackballed on many occasions when it comes to pastoring a church. The people of several churches have expressed interest in me becoming their pastor. However, the president of the district would intervene, saying they would help them to find a good pastor, one pastor to a church here in Kalamazoo that he would send fifty members to assist with tithing if they would pick one of the ministers from his church. This has happened to me three times in the city of Kalamazoo, Michigan, and twice in the surrounding cities. People have taken the process out of God's hands, and that's the reason the church is on a downtrend. I call these individuals "little Gods with no authority." I would love to build for God to open up the windows of heaven and pour out a blessing for Pastor Thomas Lockhart to pastor again, but under his leadership. I know that my heart is in the right spot. I know that I am the right person for the job. I trust in God with all my heart, soul, and mind. I have even asked God to allow me to win the lottery so that I might build a church in his name.

I simply want to be a witness for the Lord Jesus Christ. If anyone happens to read my writings and feel compelled to help me, please contact in Kalamazoo, Michigan. I am currently attending Bible Baptist Church at 1700 Drake Road, Kalamazoo, Michigan. To everyone who reads this book, young men/women, elders, I hope that it's intriguing to you to read my story. I hope it will assist many in their walk in this pilgrim journey. To God be the glory for the things he had done and will continue to do.

My story, again, is a late one *due* to me being a late bloomer. The fact that being a late bloomer came to me back in the eighties and has stuck with me until this day. I became a writer through my job at Family Court, where I worked as an intake caseworker. My job was to write reports for the judges and referees to include making recommendations to institutional placement, foster-care placement, family placement, and to gather information relevant to family history, background information, as well as any helpful information that could assist the family in making any changes they needed to make. This was the best part of my job—knowing you were doing something that would help in the life of a family.

Many people said to me that they thought it was impossible not to take the job home with me. I would always tell them that I had a home life that included my own family, not to exclude any family or client that I worked with but somehow never took the job home. I say to anyone who read my writing that family is very important. It is a way of maintaining strength, having someone to be there for you when the trials of life come upon you. I did say *when* and not *if* because trouble will come your way.

There are times you will need help when trials and tribulations come your way. I said that to say this, that life will deal you some sour situations. Life is not always a flower bed of ease. One must be ready for both the good and the bad times. The Bible says God allows it to rain on the just and the unjust. There may be times when you feel like you have to fight for your life. I've learned that it's best to prepare as you go from day to day. Don't wait until things get rough and then say, "Lord, help me." Get to know him before times get bad. Don't take the chance of not being unprepared. My brothers and sisters, as my mother would say, life is what you make it; and I've learned that you can throw in the towel when things get tough, or you can stand and fight for what you want/need, and I have found out that on most occasions you will be victorious.

There is an old hymnal that says victory is mine, that is, if I fight for it, if I go after what I want, what I need. We live in a world where I am more than a conqueror, and if I am more than a conqueror, I can keep on conquering. I have taught my children that the sky is the limit, not that they all reached the limits, but at least they know.

There is so much out there for us to learn, and the good thing about it is that it's available for everyone these days. You know, in the past, people would say if you want to hide or keep something from a black person, put it in writing. They were referring to a black person not reading. However, history teaches that if a black person was caught with a book or reading material during slavery times or even after that, in some places, bad things could happen to you. That stigma had to go a long way in the mind of a people. I tell young people to read everything you can. It can be just a little pamphlet lying around, but pick it up and read it if you can. We have come a long way as a people, but not all the way. This is not to say that the black man/woman are the only people who have had trials and tribulations but that all people have had their share of issues in this world. We've all come a long way in this world, in this life we've lived. We are not done yet. Changes will continue to take place as long as man reign on this earth. Life will deal us a hand that will make you cry when you think you should be laughing, but keep on making your stand, and things will get better.

Don't let anyone tell you what you can't do in this life. I've always told people can't can't do nothing, anyway. We can find anything we need to know. It is at our fingertips these days. We must learn to make sure we translate our negative energy into a positive energy and watch our lives began to change. If we keep a positive flow of energy in our lives, not only will we be helpful to self but to others as well.

I want to talk about love for a short while right here. Love, I found out, can carry you a long way. I want to talk about uncondi-tional love. Learning to love, no matter what the situation may be, can carry you a long way. Learning to love the way my faith teaches has been a blessing to me. For the Holy Bible teaches that God so loved the world that he gave his only begotten Son that whosoever believeth in him shall not perish but have eternal life. He included everyone and excluded no one. Despite of all I had to go through in this life, I learned to love every one of God's children. It was not hard, but I had to seek help from God. For the Bible teaches that

God is love, and love is God. I learned also that if we can obtain that God kind of love, we as people will begin to think like God, begin to move on up in life as he will direct our lives in a different way. Why? Because he loves all his children. My faith also teaches that love hides all faults. Think of it that way. That means we wouldn't have so many divorces, separations in our life, if we really loved one another as we say we do. We would be able to settle our differences and to work through more of our problems instead of the number of divorces or separations we encounter in life.

Most of the time we forget about what has been left for us to go by and begin to lean unto our own understanding. That can be the beginning of trouble. We can be our own worst enemy most of the time. But when we allow ourselves to implement the type of love that has been entrusted in us, we can move mountains. I am talking about spiritual mountains. An old song I recall my parents singing in the south was "Lord, don't move my mountains, but give me the strength to climb. Don't take away my stumbling blocks, but lead meall around." I tell you, the love of Jesus will carry you. Your faith and your trust in him mean so much if we could just learn to love one another.

I love the Bible because it carries with it what I find on the inside of me, and that's love. The Holy Bible teaches me to love my neighbors as I love myself. The question is, who is my neighbor? Well, I found that to be every one of God's children in every part of the world. All groups of people, all tribes of people. Not just the black man, not just the white man or the red man, but all of God's children. I recall a song published by A1 Green in the seventies called "L-O-V-E" is the message, and the message is love. Al said, tell everybody that love is the message, and the message is love—from the streets to the mountains and the heavens above. My final quote is, love is the message, and the message is *love*.

About the Author

As Albert King, the Blues Man, said, "I was born under a bad sign, been down since I began to crawl. If it wasn't for bad luck, I would have no luck at all."

Thomas Lockhart's parents were sharecroppers in the rural Mississippi Delta on a plantation. His father died when he was six years old. His death, as Thomas can recall, he was not allowed to attend his father's funeral due to small technical reasons, like not having the appropriate clothes to wear. They didn't have much along those lines. There were times when Thomas had to attend school with holes in his shoes and in his clothes. However, when he began to grow older, Thomas had a great ambition for baseball. He wanted to be a professional baseball player. He played in high school and was highly recognized. He attended college on a full baseball scholarship. He tore his right rotator cuff when he leaped for a line drive that caused him to sit out of baseball the rest of the season. This was during practice. Thomas's final ambition was when he moved to Kalamazoo, Michigan, in 1982. He played baseball on a team in the Kalamazoo city league, and the coach invited a professional scout to come to see him at practice. The scout said Thomas performed really well. He recalls being very quiet during the early years of his life. However, that changed when he left Mississippi. He began to receive blessings after blessings as he asked of them of God. Thomas became faithful to God and gained favor in and with him as each day went by. He seems to have an addition of authority when lifting up the name of God. It seems that other pastors and ministers were insecure and threatened when Thomas was around. His presence tends to cause others to turn him away or turn away from him. They tend to be jealous of what God has given him or what he has allowed himself to invest in him. Thomas has had some good days and some bad days; his good days outweigh his bad days.